Finding My Yip

Boomer's Tales: Book 1

by Christine Isley-Farmer

WANDERING IN THE WORDS PRESS

Cover design and illustrations by Taylor Bills.

Published by Wandering in the Words Press

WANDERING
IN THE WORDS
PRESS

Print ISBN: 978-1-7332126-6-3
Digital ISBN: 978-1-7332126-7-0
First Edition

For Jaxson and Addison

1.

Family

Mommy had just finished giving my sisters and me our tongue baths. I poked my wet head over our basket so I could hear better. Chloe sat next to Nana Weathers on a big, red fluffy box. Chloe said, "This book says Cavalier K-King Charles Spaniels were the f-favorite d-dogs of King Charles II."

"That's right, Chloe. Now stop and take a good breath before you slowly read the next sentence. This will help your stutter."

Chloe breathed in and slowly read, "King Charles walked around his palace ggrounds with them." She took another breath. "He let them sleep with him in his royal b-bedchamber." Stopping, she asked, "Did they s-sleep in the bed with the king, Nana?" Looking down at us, she said, "I don't think a k-king would want these wet p-puppies in his bed, even if they *are* c-clean." They laughed.

Chloe gave the book to Nana Weathers. "They're g-getting bigger fast."

"Chloe, look at this picture! This Cavalier looks a lot like Molly. Its coat is brown and white, and the eyes are big and round. Molly's puppies look like her. She was bred in England and has the famous brown Cavalier thumbprint on top of her head."

Chloe, looking at the picture, said, "Molly is a s-special dog and so are her p-puppies. I'm glad I c-came to live with you, Nana."

Nana Weathers put her paws around Chloe. When she did, I saw her touch a silver circle on one of them. The light from it got brighter. I had to close my eyes because the light hurt them.

Nana Weathers said, "I need to prepare dinner now. Take the dog book to your room so you can read it when you want."

Chloe jumped up and ran upstairs.

Nana Weathers called after her, "Be sure to wash your hands. It won't take long to heat up the leftovers."

In the kitchen, Nana Weathers yipped while she worked. My sisters and Mommy began to yip along with her. Their yipping made me happy. Wanting to have fun too, I tried to yip, but all I could do was move my mouth.

Chloe returned and sat next to our basket. She closed her eyes and listened to the yipping. "I wish I could s-sing like Nana." She saw I was trying to yip with them. "It's okay. I c-can't yip like I want to either." She reached over and picked me up.

"You're my f-favorite puppy, but don't tell your s-sisters," she said into my ear.

Nana Weathers came in to say dinner was ready.

"Nana, why can't he y-yip like his sisters? Would you ask Doctor S-Snow?"

"Puppies are like children. They don't develop in the same way at the same time. I'll call Doctor Snow tomorrow and make an appointment, because it's about time for all the puppies to have a check-up. We can ask him about it when we see him."

I didn't know Doctor Snow, but I was glad Chloe had asked about my yip.

2.

Problems

To take us for our checkups, Nana Weathers put my sisters and me in a gray box. It had holes on the sides and a metal door we could see out of at the front. My sisters and I almost got into a fight about which one of us would have the spot nearest the door. Carrying us outside to a large, metal blue box with four big wheels, Nana Weathers told Chloe to sit next to us in the back. "Be sure to fasten your seat belt, Chloe. I'll fasten the puppy carrier in too. You can watch them while I drive the car."

When we arrived at Doctor Snow's office, we followed him into a big room with lots of strange smells. When it was my turn to have my checkup, he looked in my ears and mouth. He lifted my tail and looked underneath it too. Patting me up and down from top to bottom, he said, "I can't see anything wrong with him. There's only one breed without a bark, and that is the Basenji. Since these are Cavalier puppies, I don't know why he hasn't begun to bark. However, I'll take a blood sample. It may give me more information. Hold on, little guy! This might hurt."

I felt a poke and almost jumped out of my fur.

"I'm s-sorry it hurt," Chloe said. "I hate to get shots." Then she asked, "Nana, can we get some ice cream? I think the p-puppies would like some too, and it might m-make him feel b-better."

"All right. I guess they deserve a treat, especially this little boy, but I think vanilla would be best for the puppies. What do you want?"

"Ch-Chocolate with s-sprinkles on top."

After my sisters and I returned home with our tummies filled with ice cream, we took a nap in our basket close to Mommy. I woke up to something ringing. Nana Weathers came into the room, picked the ringing thing up, and held it to her ear. I heard her say, "Thank you, Doctor Snow."

After she put it down, she said, "Chloe, come in here. That was Doctor Snow on the phone." Chloe came running.

Nana Weathers said, "Doctor Snow told me the blood work indicates no health problems, so I have an idea. Maybe you can spend some extra time petting and talking to him. It might help him learn to yip."

My favorite time of the day with Chloe was when she came to get me when she woke up. She'd take me out to potty. Then we'd go into the room that smelled the most like her. She'd climb up on a big, soft thing like the one I lay on in our dog basket. Sometimes she'd take a book and read something she called a poem to me.

One morning she said, "I know h-how hard it is not to have a yip. Kids at school t-tease me because I s-s-stutter. I'd like to m-make friends, b-but I'm afraid. I started to s-stutter after my p-parents died in the wreck. I love Nana, but I m-miss them s-so much."

I saw water dripping from her eyes. All I could do was lick her paw.

***

I heard Nana Weathers say, "Chloe, America's birthday is tomorrow. Would you like to go to the park across the street in the afternoon for a Fourth of July picnic?"

"Will there be f-fireworks too?" Chloe asked.

"Yes! They'll start when it gets dark. I've planned to fill a picnic basket with fried chicken, deviled eggs, potato salad, and chocolate cake. Would you like that?"

Chloe jumped up and down. "My favorite f-foods!"

***

My sniffer told me it must be America's birthday. Nana Weathers was in the kitchen. Mommy, my sisters, and I sniffed, sniffed, sniffed until she and Chloe left the house. My sisters and I had been playing and fighting over a small, soft round thing Mommy called a "ball" when suddenly we heard several bangs. Yipping at the popping and cracking, Mommy and my sisters ran around the room. Those loud bangs hurt my ears. I wet the floor.

Oops!

I lay down with my paws over my ears. My sister, the one with the louder yip, came running. "Fraidy cat!" she yipped, jumping on top of me.

Calling a dog "fraidy cat" is not funny. I wanted to yip back at her, but I couldn't.

Mommy saved the day. "Blimey!" she barked. "Leave him alone. Teasing him when he's scared is not nice."

After America's birthday, I decided I wasn't going to let my loud-yipped sister get the best of me ever again. Pretending to take a nap one afternoon, I waited for my chance. Padding around, she came sniff-sniffing near me. I sprang on top of her.

Surprised, she fell over with her paws kicking up in the air.

"What's up?" she yipped. Her white tummy was a sight to see.

Running in circles around her, I puffed out my chest and thought, *Smarty paws doesn't look so sure of herself now.* If I could've yipped when I'd jumped, it would've been even better.

3.

Surprises

Nana Weathers and Chloe sat at the kitchen table eating. Mommy, my sisters, and I watched and listened to them from our basket. Nana Weathers said, "It's such a beautiful sunny morning! I think I'll go out into the garden. My roses are in full bloom now. I'll take Molly and her puppies with me." She asked, "Chloe, would you like to come too?"

"I want to practice p-piano and finish my poem ab-bout the puppies."

"That sounds like fun. Join us when you're finished," Nana Weathers said.

Putting a floppy pink thing on her head, Nana Weathers led us outside. A big, bright yellow ball was in the sky. Nana Weathers yipped as she walked around. She put roses to her sniffer and sniffed, sniffed.

Mommy sniffed, sniffed the air and pricked up her ears. "Come on, all of you. I want to teach you how to follow a rabbit's scent."

I needed to potty, so I watched my sisters follow after her. Besides, I didn't feel like running on a full tummy. Hearing a loud whoosh above me, I looked up. Whatever it was had red feathers and tiny sticks coming from its feet. It had made the big ball disappear.

Oh no! Where can I run?

Frightened out of my fur, I wet myself and yipped, "Wheef!"

Nana Weathers must have heard the monster too. As it flew down toward me, she turned around. Her paw touched the silver circle. A flash of light from it made a bubble like the ones I'd seen Chloe making when we were in the backyard. Chloe would put a stick with a round circle on it to her mouth and breathe out. She'd say, "B-Blow away my troubles, t-tiny bubbles." The circle's light made a big bubble around me. I felt safe inside it.

Boing!

The monster hit the bubble and bounced off it. It must have been surprised because it let out a loud scream. The bubble popped.

Mommy and my sisters stopped their rabbit chasing when the monster made that noise. They came running. Mommy barked over and over, "Clear off! You better fly away and never come back here again." My sisters ran, sniff-sniffing, to make sure I was still in one piece. They jumped on me and licked me to let me know they were glad I was alive.

Chloe ran out of the house. "N-Nana, what's wrong with M-Molly? I h-heard—" She stopped when she saw my sisters on top of me licking away. "Wh-What happened?"

"It looks like we had a visit from the neighborhood hawk looking for a meal. "It's okay, Chloe. Molly saved the day with her barking. That hawk won't dare come back *here* again."

Mommy ran back to me. "What a relief! That hawk might have flown away with you in its talons. We'd never have seen you again," she barked.

As if I weren't already wet enough, Mommy gave me the biggest lick ever. After she'd finished, my sisters jumped on top of me again for another sloppy licking spree.

I was glad I was okay, but I was confused. Nana Weathers had said Mommy scared the hawk away, but I'd seen something else. If it hadn't been for that bubble, I would have been that hawk's

meal. But I had yipped! Maybe I could do it
again?

***

Ever since I'd missed being that hawk's
meal, I'd been waiting until I could find the
chance to be by myself.

"Chloe, come with me to the grocery
store. Mrs. Hayes is coming over
tomorrow," Nana Weathers said.

When they left, I padded into the
kitchen and went under the table. I tried
yipping again. "Hack. Hack. Hack." Every
time I tried to yip, I couldn't. My neck was
tight, so I gave up.

After I'd rested, words Nana Weathers
had said to Chloe came to me.

Take a good breath.

So, I took one in. A yip came out like the one I'd made in the garden.

Although I'd yipped again, I wondered, *How will anyone hear me if I can't yip louder than this?*

Sniff, sniff, sniffing, Mommy padded into the kitchen. "There you are! Son, I need to let you know we'll be leaving Mrs. Weathers and Chloe. They agreed to take care of us while our owner, Mrs. Hayes, was away on a long trip. She's coming to get us."

Surprised, I tried to yip, but my neck tightened.

Mommy barked, "I know you and Chloe are special friends. That's why I wanted to give you the news while they're gone. Chloe already knows we live somewhere else."

Hanging my head, all I could do was go to Mommy and rub my sniffer against hers.

4.
Visit

Something buzzed. Mommy barked. Nana Weathers and Chloe went to the door and let a woman in. Mommy, excited to see her, ran barking to her. The woman bent over and patted Mommy on the head and scratched behind her ears. Then Mommy ran back over to us.

"Thank you, Celia, for looking after them," Mrs. Hayes said.

"All the puppies are doing well, Nancy. We've enjoyed having them and Molly here. Come into the kitchen. I just made some fresh coffee and baked a chocolate pound cake. It's one of Chloe's favorites."

Pricking up my ears, I padded after them and lay down under the table. I wanted to hear more.

After Nana Weathers had given Mrs. Hayes her coffee and cake, Mrs. Hayes said, "Celia, I know you've been concerned about Chloe's speech. Has her stuttering improved while I was away?"

"Not really. I'm hoping with time it'll improve, but if not, I'll need to find a speech therapist."

Mrs. Hayes asked, "Do you think having a dog would help her? I can't keep *four* dogs, and I'd like to give one of the puppies to you as thanks for looking after them."

"Chloe has a special bond with the boy puppy already," Nana Weathers said.

"Well then, it's settled. Let's tell her now."

Nana Weathers called, "Chloe, come in here. Mrs. Hayes wants to ask you a question."

Chloe came running into the kitchen with Mommy and my sisters padding behind her.

Mrs. Hayes asked, "Would you like to have the boy puppy?"

"Nana, c-can I?" Chloe asked, jumping up and down.

Smiling, Nana Weathers said, "Yes, you can. Now give Mrs. Hayes a BIG hug."

Coming out from under the table, I went to Mommy and my sisters.

After she hugged Mrs. Hayes, Chloe picked me up and shouted, "I have a n-name for him. B-Boomer! He's gonna have a b-big yip."

I liked my name and the thought of having a big yip. I tried to yip to let Chloe know how happy I was. "Hack. Hack. Achoo."

"Bless you," Chloe said. "I hope you're not c-catching a cold."

Nana Weathers looked at Chloe. "Boomer is trying to let you know he likes his name. I believe he's going to have a special yip one day. All those years teaching music taught me how to recognize talent."

Mrs. Hayes laughed. "If anyone can recognize yip potential, it would be you."

In my happiness about staying with Chloe and Nana Weathers, I'd forgotten Mommy and my sisters would be leaving. Chloe took me to them and sat down next to me. She said, "I'll t-try to help you not m-miss your mom and s-sisters so much. I know how that f-feels."

After I'd licked them goodbye, Mommy barked, "Cheerio, son! Always do your best and remember your manners."

Before leaving, Mrs. Hayes bent down and patted me on the head. She said, "Boomer, how about I bring Molly and your sisters over next week for a visit?"

Although I knew they had to go, I was glad I'd see them again. As they left, I thought about what Nana Weathers had said to Mrs. Hayes.

How can she be sure I have a special yip?

5.

Discovery

Excited about what Nana Weathers had said about my yip, I worked on it when she and Chloe weren't in the house. I was still afraid to try it in front of them though.

Chloe would usually come home while I could still see the big yellow ball outside. She'd run up the stairs to her room. I was always waiting for her in my basket. My front paws hung over the top of it.

Chloe had noticed. "Boomer needs a b-bigger bed to sleep in," she told Nana Weathers.

"You're right, Chloe. He's eating so much that he's growing by leaps and bounds. He'd be more comfortable sleeping if he had a larger bed. I'll go to Pet Friend."

After Nana Weathers left, Chloe said, "Let's play a pretend g-game." She picked me up and placed me on her bed. "I'm a q-queen. Everyone has to like me and do what I s-say." Looking at me, she said, "You're my loyal s-subject. I want you to l-lay down." Chloe raised her paws up and down.

Not sure what she wanted, I lay down and pretended to sleep. She sat next to me, so I opened one eye to look at her. I saw water in her eyes. "I used to have friends before I c-came here, but I can't seem to m-make them now," she said.

I licked her paw, but that didn't seem to help. So I took a long, slow breath and yipped, "Wheef!"

"B-Boomer, y-y-you yipped!" She picked me up and ran around her room singing, "Boomer found his yip t-today. Run, jump, skipping we'll p-play." Suddenly, she stopped and said, "I want to s-sing, but my st-st . . ."

Nana Weathers came into the room with what looked like a new bed for me. "What's going on?"

Chloe set me down and brushed her paw across her eyes. "Boomer c-can yip."

"I'm not surprised. Didn't I tell you he might begin to yip if you spent time with him? Chloe, show Boomer his new bed so he can try it on for size. I hope it's roomy enough. The tan and black colors should go nicely with his coat."

In my bed, I sniff, sniffed and circled round and round. Diggity, diggity, digging, I found the perfect spot to lie down. I rolled over on my back, kicking my paws up in the air to let Nana Weathers know how comfy it was. I yipped, "Wheef! Wheef!"

"Well, what do you know! Boomer has let me hear him yip too," Nana Weathers said. "This calls for a wonderful surprise for you both. While I was at Pet Friend, I saw a flyer for obedience classes. Since Boomer is old enough for a beginner's course, I thought this might be a good idea. I've enrolled you two. You should be his training partner, Chloe, but I'll be there to watch and learn as well."

Excited, I leapt out of my bed and ran to Chloe. When she reached down to pick me up, her paws were shaking. Hugging me against her, she took a deep breath and said, "Okay."

6.
Friends

Nana Weathers let us off in front of Pet Friend. "It shouldn't take me long to find a parking place," she said. "Go on inside to the training room in the back."

Chloe and I went into the store where I sniff-sniffed lots of different things. She was leading me on my new red leash Nana Weathers had purchased with my bed. A black-haired boy, leading a small gray dog, bumped into us. "Sorry, he said."

Suddenly, his gray dog pulled away from him.

Zap!

He kicked me.

He raced out of the training room. Remembering my loud-yipped sister, I wasn't going to let him get away with kicking me, so I pulled away from Chloe and ran after him.

Gray dog was too fast for me. He stopped and looked back. "C'mon, man. Let's grab some toys and play."

Panting, I stopped to catch my breath. I heard a loud voice say, "Customers, today's special is thirty percent off any dry dog and cat foods on aisles nine and ten. Limit is two bags per customer. Hurry to be sure you don't lose out on a great deal. It will only last ten minutes." Pushing big silver carriers on wheels, customers all ran in the same direction. There were so many different scents, I couldn't smell gray dog anymore.

A large yellow box on top of big wheels with a man seated on top went beep-beep-beeping down one of the store aisles.

Uh oh!

Gray dog had been running that way.

Chloe and the black-haired boy ran up to me. She grabbed my leash. "Your d-dog ran that way," she said, pointing.

Shouting "Hoppy, Hoppy, Hoppy," the boy ran toward that aisle. We followed him and got there in time to hear him yell, "Stop!" The man behind the window must have heard him too, because the box screeched to a stop. The boy picked up Hoppy, held up his paw, and said, "Thanks!"

He came back to us. "Hi. My name is Robbie Goodson. Thanks for helping me. I was scared something bad was gonna happen to Hoppy. That loader could've hit him."

Chloe looked down at the floor, so I yipped, "Wheef."

"What's your dog's name?" he asked.

"B-Boomer. I'm Chloe W-Weathers."

Robbie said, "Hoppy is a mixed breed. Mom and Dad adopted him from an animal shelter a couple of months ago. They wanted me to have a friend."

"N-Nana let me have Boomer for the s-same reason."

Nana Weathers ran up to us. "It took me longer than I thought to find a parking place. When you weren't in the training room, I got worried."

"Nana, this is R-Robbie and his d-dog Hoppy."

Smiling at them, Nana Weathers said, "Nice to meet you. Why are all of you out here?"

Robbie told her about the loader. "Hoppy is frisky and gets into trouble a lot. Mom and Dad thought obedience classes would be a good idea."

Hoppy looked at me and yipped, "Yeah. That's what they think."

I yipped back to him, "Could be fun."

"Jump shot, man! You need to toss that yip up higher. With all the noise in this place, I can't hear ya," he yipped.

Nana Weathers said, "Boomer is well behaved, but I thought the class would be a good way for Chloe and him to become a better team."

"Mom and Dad said the same thing. Hey, I've got an idea." Looking at Chloe, Robbie asked, "Would you like to practice together outside of class too?"

Chloe smiled and said, "Sure."

"Let's head back to the training room now. You two can exchange phone numbers and addresses at the end of class," Nana Weathers said.

I wasn't sure how I felt about training with Hoppy. He reminded me a little too much of my loud-yipped sister.

7.

Practice

In our backyard, Chloe and I were practicing what we'd learned in our last class. "Great job signaling, Chloe," Nana Weathers said. "Boomer sat right away when you held your palm up."

"He deserves a t-treat," Chloe said, reaching into her bag. I wagged my tail in agreement.

"Well, I'll leave you two to it," Nana Weathers said. "I need to start dinner. I'm sure Robbie and Hoppy will be joining you soon. Chloe, try to practice the spoken commands too. I know you're nervous about saying them in class, but Boomer needs to learn both."

"I know, Nana. I'll t-try." Chloe looked at me. She turned her palm over and said, "Boomer, down." Then she gave me another treat. I liked this game.

Robbie ran into the backyard tugging Hoppy on his leash. "Sorry we're late. I had to look for Hoppy. He was hiding under my bed. I had to crawl underneath and pull him out. Mom'll be back in an hour or so to pick us up."

"We've only been p-practicing a little while," Chloe said. "B-Boomer has learned to sit every time I g-give him the palm up s-signal."

"Hoppy doesn't like to sit, but if I point my finger to my eye, he watches me, because I give him a treat *and* throw his ball," Robbie said. "He loves to run after it. I wish he'd bring it back too." They laughed.

Chloe said, "Let's p-practice the hand s-signal for come. M-Maybe Hoppy will b-bring the ball back if I throw it to Boomer first."

As loud as my yip would let me, I yipped to Hoppy, "You'd give Robbie a yummy treat if you'd listen and do the commands. You don't fool me; you know them too."

He yipped back, "Yeah? The only good thing about training classes is the treats I get there, but the ones I get at home are yucky."

Chloe and Robbie came to us. Chloe had my red ball in her hand. She held her palm up. "Sit," she said. When I did, she threw the ball.

Whoosh!

I ran after it. As soon as I had it in my mouth, she signaled me to sit again.

Chloe pointed to her eye. I watched as she placed her hand across her chest. I ran back to her. Her treat bag slipped from her hand, and some treats tumbled to the ground. Hoppy ran fast, faster, fastest

toward those treats and gobbled them up.
Chloe laughed and picked up the bag.

Licking his chops, Hoppy yipped, "Man,
those treats beat hamburger!"

It was Hoppy's turn next. Robbie said,
"Hoppy, sit." He showed Hoppy the hand
signal too.

Chloe said, "G-give him one of these t-
treats now." She handed the bag to Robbie.

Hoppy sat and Robbie gave him the
treat. Robbie said, "Good dog."

Robbie threw the ball, and Hoppy
grabbed it up. Robbie gave him the hand
signal to sit, which Hoppy did.

Chloe said, "Hold up the b-bag of treats and shake it, Robbie."

Shaking and holding it up for Hoppy to see, Robbie shouted, "Hoppy, come!"

Hoppy couldn't run back fast enough with the ball. He dropped it at Robbie's feet. After jumping up and down, Robbie bent to scratch Hoppy's ears. He gave him a treat, and said, "That's my champ."

"You sure made Robbie happy," I yipped.

"Man, when Robbie gets excited watching a basketball game, he jumps up and down and shouts, 'Three-pointer' like the one I just scored."

Chloe said, "Hoppy s-seems to like these treats. T-Take the rest of these. I've got another b-bag inside. I'll s-show you where Nana found them at Pet Friend."

Nana Weathers opened the back door. "Hey, it's getting dark. Time to come in. Hi there, Robbie and Hoppy. Robbie, your mother just called; she's on her way."

Before going into the house, I yipped to Hoppy, "Let's go for more three-pointers for Robbie and Chloe in the next training class."

8.

Peanut

Bob, our trainer, stood at the front of the room. He said, "Owners, take your dogs to the wall. We're going to practice a new command today. I'll come around to each of you and throw a toy to your dog. You'll give the command to leave it, then pull your dog by its leash away from the toy. When your dog understands the command and doesn't go after the toy, give it a treat."

Bob went around to all the dogs in the room several times. Each one of us was able to understand the command and do it, so Bob said, "Let's move on to the next stage. I'm going to throw a toy to the middle of the room. When I do, let go of your dogs' leashes and give the command to leave it."

When Bob threw the toy to the middle of the room, Jack, a boy who was bigger than Chloe and Robbie, told his dog, Peanut, to leave it. But Peanut ran growling and barking to the middle of the room, He yipped, "Stay out of my way. This toy is mine." He picked the toy up, shaking it from side to side. None of us, even if we'd forgotten the command, would have run to the middle of the room. We knew Peanut was a bully and would have fought us for that toy if we did.

Peanut's behavior got worse as our classes went on. He wet the floor if we got close to him. He'd yip, "You think you're the top dog here. Well, I've got news for you. I may be a Chihuahua, but I'm the big shot in this class. Get out of my way. This space is mine." All of us tried to stay as far away as possible.

Bob sometimes cleaned up Peanut's messes, but after Peanut continued to have bad manners, he said to Jack, "I need you to clean up after your dog when he makes a mess on the floor. I must pay more attention to the rest of the dogs."

Doogie, who said he was a German Shepherd puppy, was afraid of Peanut. During one class, he pulled away from his owner. Running out of the room, tail tucked between his legs, he yipped, "Take me home—I can't stand this pipsqueak anymore." To see a dog much larger than Peanut running away wasn't funny.

Even though Chloe and Robbie kept practicing with Hoppy and me after school, Chloe was still having trouble saying the commands without stuttering. In class, she only wanted to give me hand signals. Bob reminded her to say and do the hand signals together whenever possible.

In one class, Chloe had to speak. Bob explained how it went. "Your dogs will understand how important this command is by the sound and volume of your voice. If you think your dog is in danger or lost, use your highest and loudest voice to call its name over and over. Chloe, you and Boomer will be the first pair to do the exercise."

All of us went out of the training room into the store. Robbie led me down a long aisle. When Chloe called, he was supposed to drop my leash. Bob said, "Chloe, call Boomer. You can't see him—he's lost."

In a loud, clear voice, Chloe shouted, "Boomer!" She repeated my name over and over without stuttering. When I reached her side, she petted me and said, "Good boy, Boomer!" I got my favorite treat.

"I hope all of you were paying attention," Bob said. "That was a perfect example of how this command should be given." Chloe gave me a big smile.

***

"We only have one more c-class before graduation day," Chloe told Robbie. "I'm n-nervous. I hope I don't f-forget any of the commands and s-signals."

"You've been doing great in class, Chloe. Your commands are much louder, and we've been working lots outside of class too. I bet we'll pass."

Hoppy and I had also been yipping to one another about graduation day—but for another reason.

Hoppy yipped, "I think I've finally warmed up to this training thing. But I can't take much more of Peanut. I thought I had problems, but he's a hard nut to crack."

"I think I might have a plan to bring Peanut down to his real size," I yipped. "Can you help me?"

55

"You bet. I don't think Doogie and the others can take much more. We're ready to chew off one of that pig-headed little guy's ears."

I yipped my plan into Hoppy's ear as loud as possible.

"Heard you loud and clear, man! I wish I'd thought of that, 'cause you've got a slam dunk here. I'll help get the word out to the other dogs at our next class."

***

Graduation day was here. Nana Weathers, Mr. and Mrs. Goodson, and Robbie's sister,

Ella, sat in chairs in the training room with others watching us do our exercises. So far, things had gone well.

"Owners, this is your last graduation day exercise," Bob said. "Take your dogs on their leashes to the opposite wall, drop their leashes, and tell your dogs to sit." Once our owners had done it, Bob said, "Give your dogs the hand signal to stay. Then return to this side of the room."

Peanut sat next to me. When our owners called our names and told us to come, I looked over at him.

He yipped, "I've had it! No more playing nicey-nicey." He lay down and rolled over on his back. The rest of us ran to our owners.

Bob's face turned red, but he said, "Let's try this once more. Take your dogs to the other end of the room and give them the same commands. Return back here."

Jack followed the other owners and dogs back to the wall. He made Peanut stand up. Giving him the commands to sit and stay, he said, "One last chance."

Bob said, "Call your dogs!"

I saw a flash of light. Peanut jumped up. Recognizing the light had come from Nana Weathers's silver circle and with no time to spare, I grabbed Peanut's leash with my teeth. Hoppy shot out to the center of the room. The other dogs ran to Peanut's sides and formed a doggy fence. Standing in front of Peanut with his teeth bared, Hoppy dared him not to follow. "Just try any shenanigans, and I'll dribble you all the way down this court."

I kept pulling Peanut's leash and the other dogs closed in; he had no choice but to follow. At Jack's feet, Peanut lay down and yipped, "I give up, brainiacs. You win."

Excited, Doogie barked, "Whoopee!" He made a *big* puddle right next to Peanut's sniffer.

We were excited about our graduation from obedience classes. Even Jack and

Peanut had made it through. But I knew why Peanut had followed me. I planned to diggity-dig-dig until I found out more about Nana Weathers's silver circle.

9.
Music Room

I was in my favorite corner of the kitchen chewing on my rope toy, when the back door opened. I jumped up and yipped, "Wheef," when Nana Weathers came in. She'd come back from taking Chloe to school.

She was holding a green round thing with tiny metal legs sitting on top of a long stick. She closed, opened, and shook it. The shaking reminded me of my baths. Chloe would put me in water and rub me with something she called soap. After she was done, she'd wrap me in a soft thing and move it back and forth on my fur before letting me go. I'd run around her room as fast as I could. When I ran, she'd laugh and say, "You're doing the sh-shake, shake dance."

"I'm glad my umbrella was in the car, Boomer. It started to rain as soon as I dropped Chloe off in front of the school entrance. The weatherman on the car radio said it was going to rain the rest of the day. Since it's not a good day for a walk, this would be a good time to show you the music room where Chloe practices piano."

She led me to a door, and when she opened it, her silver circle was glowing. My ears wiggle-waggled and buzzed.

"Boomer, welcome to the music room! I heard your yip getting stronger during obedience classes, so I think you're ready to learn how to sing."

Nana Weathers sang something I'd heard her sing before in the kitchen. Excited, I sat up on my hind legs with my front paws up, took a deep breath, and yipped as loudly as I could, "Wheef! Wheef!"

"After I pick Chloe up from school, we'll come in here again. Now, I need to wash up the breakfast dishes, do some laundry, and other rainy-day chores. While I'm busy, you can go up to Chloe's room."

When she closed the door to the music room, her silver circle no longer glowed, and my ears had stopped wiggling and buzzing. I padded up the stairs and lay down in my bed. The room's warmth and my comfy bed made me sleepy. As I closed my eyes, my paws began to twitch like they do when Chloe and I begin to play a game in my sleep.

We are in Chloe's bathroom after my bath and "sh-shake, shake" dance.

"Nana told me it'll soon be t-time to start b-brushing your teeth. Since your teeth are s-small, Nana will b-brush them for you. B-But I want you to watch me brush mine f-first to see how it's done." Standing at a big bowl, she reaches for something that looks like a white stick with white fur sticking up on it.

"I p-put toothpaste on my t-toothbrush, wet it with water, and b-brush my teeth like this." She moves the toothbrush up down, up down, and side to side on her teeth. "Then I f-fill a cup with water and s-swish the water and toothpaste around in my m-mouth. After that, I spit it into the s-sink."

Chloe opens her mouth and shows me her teeth that are white like her toothbrush.

I hear a voice calling me from the distance. "Boomer, Boomer, wake up."

I opened my eyes. "I hope you had a pleasant dream while you napped," said Nana Weathers. She was rubbing my tummy. "I'm leaving to pick Chloe up from school."

***

When Chloe had finished her after-school snack, Nana Weathers said, "I showed Boomer the music room this morning. I thought you might like to play the piano for him."

I went to Chloe and tugged at her skirt.

"Nana, you're right. He wants to g-go in there again."

Chloe opened the music room door. She walked to a big black box and sat down in front of it. "Boomer, come."

I padded to her.

"This is the piano; I love to p-play it." Chloe raised her arms and hands; her fingers ran up and down it. I heard the same tinkling I'd heard before when she was in here. The piano and Chloe were playing a game.

Wanting to be nearer to join in the fun, I padded closer and sat. I saw the piano had teeth too, but some of them were black. I yipped, "The piano needs a toothbrush too!"

While Chloe played, Nana Weathers sat down in a chair that moved forwards backwards, forwards backwards. She closed her eyes. Her silver circle glowed; my ears wiggle-waggled and buzzed again.

Opening her eyes, Nana Weathers touched her silver circle. A flash of light made me stand up—just as it had done with Peanut. She asked, "Chloe, would you play a song for me? It's one you know." Nana

Weathers stood and picked up some papers from a table. She handed them to Chloe.

I sat and listened to the song. Nana Weathers touched her circle again. From it came sparkling little lights. They circled up and down around me. I wanted to yip with Nana Weathers. Breathing in, I yipped, "Wheef. Wheef. Wheef."

When the song ended, the lights disappeared. My ears stopped wiggling and buzzing.

Chloe jumped up. "Nana, B-B-Boomer was y-yipping with you!"

"He just needed some encouragement. His little yip sounds nice, doesn't it? I'll work with him during the day while you're at school. Will you play piano again for him when he's improved? I think you two would make a good musical team."

10.
Yip Lessons

Nana Weathers led me into the music room and sat down at the piano. Her circle was glowing. "Let's warm up your yip. Warming up before you and Chloe practice is important." She touched her circle. The sparkling lights from it felt like Chloe's fingers scratch-scratching behind my ears.

Placing her hands on the piano, Nana Weathers said, "I'll be singing different pitches, so listen first and then yip after me. Begin with all fours on the floor. Find your balance over each paw and hold your head and nose up. Remember to take a good breath in before each pitch you yip."

I was having fun with this game. My yip started to taste like that vanilla ice cream Chloe had given me after seeing Doctor Snow. The more I yipped, the warmer and sweeter it became.

"Boomer, you're a fast learner," Nana Weathers said. "Your yip sounds better already. Tomorrow we can work on some more exercises, but that's enough for today." Her circle stopped glowing; the lights faded. "I think you deserve a new kind of treat as a reward. Bob told me about these special biscuits that are all the rage with dogs."

Quickly padding into the kitchen after her, I yipped, "Bring on those biscuits! I can't wait for my next lesson."

***

Whenever Nana Weathers was busy and Chloe was in school, I'd pad up to Chloe's room to warm up my yip. I was still having trouble with my higher yips. Nana Weathers had said, "Be careful not to tighten or push for your high notes."

From the bottom of the stairs, Nana Weathers called, "Bye, Boomer. I'll be back soon. I have an errand to run, and then I'm picking Chloe up from school."

I began to practice after I heard the door close. Wanting to try some of my higher yips, I yipped one, which felt good. But the next one I tried wasn't as loud. I wanted it to be as good as the first one, so I yipped it over and over. The last one cracked. Thinking I should probably practice some lower yips too, I yipped. *Nothing* came out. I tried again and again, but my yip was gone.

I heard Nana Weathers and Chloe talking when they came into the house. When I didn't run down the stairs wag-wagging my tail, Chloe came to me. I was lying in my bed with my head tucked between my paws.

"Boomer, what's w-wrong? Nana, come q-quickly! S-Something is wrong with B-Boomer."

Nana Weathers came upstairs. Looking me up and down, she said, "We'll take him to see Doctor Snow right now to find out what's the matter with him."

I tried to yip a thank you, but all I could do was move my mouth. I shook with fright. I hadn't felt like this since I'd been scared of those "f-fireworks" and the hawk.

In the examination room, the doctor looked me over. Thank goodness he didn't get out that needle. Finally, he said, "Boomer looks healthy to me. There's some discharge in his ears that may be due to allergy. Put these drops in twice a day. If his ears don't get better in a couple of weeks, bring him back."

Chloe asked, "W-What about his yip?"

"Sometimes dogs develop allergies that affect their barks. If I'm right, when the ears clear up, he should be able to yip again."

Back in the car, I was calmer but still worried I might not be able to yip anymore.

Chloe put the drops in my ears twice a day. I overheard Nana Weathers tell her, "Boomer likes to practice his yip during the day when you're at school. He may have pushed it too much. There'll be no more yip lessons for the time being. We'll need to let his yip rest and the medicine do its job."

11.

Encounter

After Chloe had given me the last of my ear drops, Nana Weathers said to her, "Some fresh air and sunshine might be good for Boomer. Why don't you take him for a walk in the park across the street today?"

"I'll c-call Robbie and ask him if he wants to b-bring Hoppy and go with us," Chloe said.

As Hoppy and I sniff-sniffed our way along the path, Robbie said, "Uh oh! It's Joey and Ezra." He pointed to two boys on top of boards with small round wheels.

"Joey makes fun of me because I like math. I don't like being around him."

"He's p-probably jealous of your good grades," Chloe said. "By the way, I like m-math too. I'm s-sorry he hurts your feelings. He and Ezra t-tease me about my stutter, s-so I know how you feel. If I try to s-say something back, I can't."

"We better go before they reach us," Robbie said.

Before we could turn to head back to Chloe's house, the boys came to a stop in front of us. "Hey look, Ezra. It's nerd head and his girlfriend, one of them said."

The boy laughed and pointed at Hoppy and me. "And their stupid dogs."

Hoppy and I looked at each other. We were both thinking of Peanut. Hoppy growled.

"Take that back about our dogs!" Chloe said.

That's when the other boy spoke. "Well, what d'ya know. G-G-Girlfriend can talk."

Hoppy pulled at his leash until it slipped out of Robbie's hands. Then his teeth gripped onto the boy called Joey's pants and tugged.

Joey's face got red, and he balled up his hands. I thought he was going to hit Robbie. Moving to avoid a hit, Robbie also tried to grab Hoppy's leash.

Robbie shouted, "Hoppy, leave it!" Hoppy kept tugging.

I didn't think Ezra wanted to play this game, but I also wasn't sure he wouldn't help Joey. I had to do something. I'd been resting my yip, so I wondered if I could yip loud enough for someone to hear. I lifted my head, nose pointing up. With all fours on the ground, I breathed in and yipped, "Woof! Woof! Woof!"

Nana Weathers must have heard me, because she came out of the house and ran to the edge of the park. Her silver circle glowed brightly. She made her lips into whistle lips. Instead of whistling like she would sometimes do to call me, out of her mouth came a strong wind. Trees in the park moved back and forth. Leaves fell to the ground. Hoppy let go of Joey's pants. Everyone looked around to see what was happening.

Joey shouted, "Hey Ezra, let's get outta here. This park's kinda spooky."

They couldn't get on their boards fast enough. As they rolled away, Chloe and Robbie laughed.

Nana Weathers ran up to us. "What happened?"

Robbie said, "Hoppy didn't rip off Joey's pant leg, Chloe told him not to call our dogs stupid, I avoided getting punched, and it looks like Boomer has his yip back. That's all."

Nana Weathers laughed. "How would you two like some freshly baked chocolate chip cookies? I've even got some special doggy biscuits for Boomer and Hoppy."

I yipped at Hoppy, "Those biscuits Bob recommended are the best."

"Hey man, next to watching basketball with Robbie, you know eating's my favorite sport. Let's go!"

As I followed Hoppy, I wondered what other things Nana Weathers and her silver circle could do.

12.
Debut

After breakfast one morning, Nana Weathers said, "Chloe, it's been a few weeks now since Boomer got back his yip. I think he's ready for a small audience. It would be good experience for him to perform."

I thought, *Depends on who'd be listening.*

"Robbie and Hoppy! They're our b-best friends. Let's s-surprise them. I haven't told Robbie Boomer c-can sing."

Jumping up into Chloe's lap, I yipped, "Tummy full of yummy treats!"

Chloe said, "I'll invite them over after s-school."

When Nana Weathers returned from taking Chloe to school, she led me in into the music room. She said, "I want to tell you about my ring."

My ears pricked up. She touched her silver circle.

"This ring, when I have it on my finger, makes it possible for us to understand one another and for you to sing. It was given to me by my grandmother, who told me its wearer can perform all kinds of magic. My grandmother warned me to be careful when, where, and how I used its power. She said, 'When you're not wearing it, keep it safe. In wrong hands, it can be capable of evil things.'"

By this time, I'd begun to pant, pant, pant with excitement.

"You're the only one who has been able to see the ring's magic, Boomer. Grandmother said, 'Only allow those you fully trust to see its power.'"

"But what about Chloe?" I yipped.

"Chloe isn't ready. Its power would be too strong for her now, but she'll have my ring one day. Boomer, I believe I hear Mrs. Goodson's car dropping off Chloe and our guests."

We left the music room quickly. Greeting everyone at the front door, Nana Weathers said, "I know Chloe has told you she has a surprise for you. First, let's go into the kitchen. You can have something to eat and drink before the surprise is revealed."

Chloe was excited. She gobbled down her brownie and drank her milk at top speed.

Hoppy yipped, "Hey man, what's going on with Chloe? She's as nervous as a player trying to make the winning free throw."

"Just wait. Perk up your ears when we go into the music room."

After Robbie had finished eating, Chloe asked, "Nana c-can we go into the music room now?" Without waiting for an answer, she grabbed Robbie's arm. "Come on, Robbie. You're not gonna b-believe this!" She showed Robbie to a chair.

Robbie said, "Hoppy, sit."

Grabbing some papers, Chloe said, "Boomer, come!"

I ran to stand in front of the piano like we'd practiced. My heart was beating thumpity-thump, thump.

Nana Weathers stood in the back of the room.

When Chloe began to play, Nana Weathers touched her ring. Sparkling, warm light circled around me. My buzzing ears wiggle-waggled, as I yipped with Chloe's playing.

Robbie's eyes got big. Hoppy's ears pricked up. As we neared the end of the song, Nana Weathers made her whistle lips. The wind she blew was like the soft thing Chloe rubbed me with after my bath. My fur moved with her wind and the music. As we came to the end of the song, Nana Weathers stopped blowing the wind. I jumped up on my hind legs, opened my chest, and stretched out my front paws to sing my high note like we'd practiced.

Silence.

Robbie, jumping to his feet, put his hands together over and over. He said, "Wow! That was cool. I've never heard a dog sing before."

Didn't he notice I couldn't yip my high note? I wondered.

Hoppy ran in circles around me. "Man, you're a yipping phenom!"

Hanging my head, I yipped, "Thanks."

Robbie ran to Chloe and said, "You and Boomer *have* to be in the school talent show!"

"I'm not s-sure about that," she said.

"You'll be a hit. I can't wait to see everyone's faces when they hear Boomer."

"It *would* be a good experience for him to perform somewhere besides this house," Nana Weathers said. "I have an idea, Chloe. Since you write poetry, why don't you write a poem, and I'll set it to music. What do you say? We'll work together to teach Boomer."

"B-But he won't be able to y-yip the words."

"The school's auditorium has a screen above the stage. We can project your poem onto it."

Chloe said, "I don't want t-to sing."

"I know," Nana Weathers said. "After you write the poem, you can practice saying the words in rhythm with the melody. While you play the accompaniment, you can speak the words and breathe where

Boomer breathes. Practicing this way will help you stay together."

"But what if I s-stutter?"

"I'll practice singing the words with you while you speak them. If you stammer, you can catch up with us."

With her eyes looking down at her feet, Chloe finally looked up and said, "I'll d-do it for Boomer."

13.

Struggle

Chloe had finished her poem, and Nana Weathers had set it to music. When we practiced, Chloe sometimes stuttered, but it was getting better. I noticed she'd hum and say the words along with Nana Weathers.

One afternoon Chloe came rushing up to her room. Throwing her backpack on the bed, she walked back and forth, back and forth around her room. Her steps were loud.

Nana Weathers must have heard them, because she came upstairs. "Honey, what's the matter?"

Chloe looked at her and said, "I'm n-nervous about the t-talent show. It's only a f-few days away. I'm tired of b-being teased about my,"—she paused to breath—"stutter."

"You're such a brave girl, and it has been a difficult time for you," Nana Weathers said. "I've been thinking about getting you a speech therapist to help with your stutter. Would you be willing to see one?"

She went to Nana Weathers and hugged her. The ring was glowing.

"Chloe, you don't have to perform in the talent show if you don't want to. Boomer will understand."

"Boomer s-sounds great, but I'm not s-sure if I'm good enough," she said.

"One thing I learned as a musician is that preparation is the most important part of performing. You, Boomer, and I have practiced almost every day for the past month. Both of you know the song well, and Boomer is more confident singing his higher notes. You'll have to decide if you're willing to take a chance on performing outside our house. The problem is not ability or preparation; it's confidence."

As Nana Weathers spoke, her ring glowed brighter.

Chloe looked at me. I yipped, "Come on. Let's go for a big meaty bone."

***

Nana Weathers called to Chloe from the bottom of the stairs. "You don't want to be late for school. Today is talent show day. I've made your favorite breakfast of waffles with chocolate chips on top and bacon."

I was sitting at the back door when she looked at me. "Boomer, you need to go outside to do your business, but once you're back in, I'll have something special for you too."

She didn't need to tell me that, because I'd sniffed, sniffed the chicken she was putting into my bowl with my kibble.

Chloe was sitting at the table when I came back in. She said, "Nana, I've got b-butterflies in my s-stomach. I'm not very hungry."

I was feeling like that too, especially about my high notes. I lay down beside my bowl.

"Nerves are a natural part of performing," Nana Weathers said. "I used to be nervous on the day of a performance too. What helped me was to find some time alone during the day. I'd sit and think about the songs and their words. I'd ask myself, *What are the emotions in the words and music I most want to share with others?*"

I noticed Chloe had started to eat something while she listened. I was feeling better too, so I went for the chicken in my bowl.

"Chloe, music is very powerful. It's a gift we share with others. When we do, listeners understand. The music speaks through us to them."

Chloe stopped eating. She went to Nana Weathers and hugged her. "I love you, Nana."

With her ring glowing, Nana Weathers said, "I love you too. Now finish your breakfast. Boomer, you can come along with me to drop Chloe off at school."

At the school, Nana waved goodbye to Chloe. Then she turned to me. "How about a walk today? I just happened to bring along your leash. Some exercise will do us good."

After our walk, Nana Weathers said, "Let's sit and rest for a moment." She told me to jump up on the bench beside her. As she talked, her ring glowed. "Boomer, I'm going to need your help at the talent show. Although we don't use them anymore, I

know you remember the hand signals you
learned in obedience classes. I'm counting
on you to follow them tonight, no matter
what."

Sitting up on my haunches, I yipped,
"More of those yummy biscuits?" I reached
my right paw to touch her hand.

She shook it and said, "It's a deal."

14.
Talent Show

Chloe and I stood behind the red curtain on the New Hope Elementary School stage. Nana Weathers said, "Chloe, I got this velvet ribbon for your hair. It'll match your blue dress. Boomer, I hope you like the red bowtie to go with your little black and white tuxedo."

While she tied Chloe's ribbon, I yipped, "I love my tuxedo. I feel like a king. Why, I *am* a king."

There were lots of performers. Elsie Charles leapt up and down. Turning, turning, turning, Elsie made me dizzy.

Shannon Grace blew on a long, shiny metal tube with holes in it. *She's good*, I thought. The animal acts made me sniff-sniff.

Chloe, watching, pointed and said, "That's f-funny. Russell Ellis's hamster, Ernie, is running as f-fast as he can on a wheel while Russell plays his d-drum."

My favorite animal act was when Danny McBride pulled a white rabbit out of a tall black hat.

It's good that I've been to obedience classes, I thought. My nose was telling me to run, run, run after that rabbit.

Maggie Price threw a big, shiny stick with red, white, and blue things on it high up in the air. She caught and threw that stick over and over. When it fell to the floor, I had to stop myself from fetching it.

Chloe walked back and forth, wiggling her fingers and hands. I had a return of butterflies, but I was remembering to take deep breaths like Nana Weathers had told me to do. I went over to Chloe. She looked down at me and said, "It'll soon be t-time for us."

"We're ready," I yipped.

Nana Weathers came over and said, "Everything with the screen has been arranged. I'm going out. I'll stand in the back of the auditorium to make sure the projector's focus is clear." She gave Chloe a kiss, and me a pat on the head. "Have fun. Let the music speak through you."

Finally, it was time for me and Chloe to go on. Mr. Fellows, the principal said, "Welcome to the stage Chloe Weathers and her singing dog, Boomer. They'll be performing a song composed by Mrs. Celia Weathers with words by Chloe."

I went out first and walked to the front of the stage. Chloe followed. Nana Weathers had said, "When the audience claps, both of you must bow together." I stretched my front legs and paws forward to take a bow with Chloe. She sat down at the piano. Robbie, Ella, and their parents sat in front of us.

Before Chloe started playing the piano, I started to worry about my highest note. I had to hold it longer than any of the others. What if I cracked or couldn't sing it?

At the back of the auditorium, I saw the ring's light get brighter as its sparkling lights circled down and around me. My ears wiggle-waggled, as I yipped the pitches set to Chloe's poem:

> *My heavy heart could find no rest.*
> *It sadly beat within my chest.*
> *It could not hope or understand,*

My highest note was on the second word of the next line. I remembered what Nana Weathers had said about letting the music speak through you.

Till Peace touched it with its gentle hand.

My high note came out sweet as vanilla ice cream. As Chloe continued to play between the verses, the light from the ring faded. Not knowing what to do next, I saw Nana Weathers give me the hand signals for sit and stay.

For the second verse, I looked back at Chloe. She didn't seem to notice I was no longer singing. A white light glowed above her head.

Sweet music sounds from far away;
Birds tweet and twitter all the day.
My heart is filled with tenderness;
A love for life brings me happiness.

Chloe's voice was sweet and clear. Not once did she stutter. At the end of our song, there was silence. When Robbie started to clap, everyone joined in and stood up.

After the talent show, Mr. and Mrs. Goodson and Ella came over to our house for a party. Robbie had asked if he could bring Hoppy along.

Nana Weathers greeted everyone at the door. "Come in and have some refreshments. I've made chicken salad sandwiches and ham biscuits, so please help yourselves. There're chips, nuts, grapes, and chocolate cupcakes too."

Hoppy and my noses were busy sniff-sniffing all the different things on the table. Nana Weathers noticed. "I haven't forgotten you two. I've put some doggy biscuits and chicken into two bowls."

As we padded off toward the kitchen, I stopped when I heard Mrs. Goodson say, "Chloe, you're a talented young girl with a lovely voice."

"Thank you."

"And I've never heard a dog bark like that before," said Mr. Goodson. "His barking was one of a kind. Chloe, your poem was touching. I'm happy you and Boomer won first place."

"Nana, Boomer, and I practiced almost every day to get ready," Chloe said. "We worked as a team."

Robbie said, "Do you know you didn't stutter when you sang?"

"No, I wasn't thinking about s-singing. I was feeling the music."

Nana Weathers gave her a hug.

Hoppy yipped, "Man, I heard you took a timeout in the last quarter."

"I was doing what was best for the team," I yipped back.

As Hoppy and I started again to pad into the kitchen, Chloe called, "Come, Boomer!"

I ran to her. She reached down to pick me up.

She said into my ear, "You're my best f-friend always. Thanks for helping me find *my* yip."

The End

Sniffing Out Funtastic Facts

Cavalier King Charles Spaniels, named for King Charles II who ruled England from 1649–1660, were a popular toy breed with the British aristocracy. Charles loved the breed so much he made his brother, King James II, promise to continue breeding them. When Charles died in 1685, twelve spaniels grieved at his bedside. Even though their popularity lessened after Charles's death, they still remained favorite dogs on country estates and warmed the laps of aristocratic ladies. As a young girl, Victoria, who became queen in 1837, owned a Cavalier she named Dash.

Basenji is a hunting dog that originated in central Africa. It is commonly placed in the hound group in English-speaking countries. Basenjis produce a yodel-like sound, which is called a "baroo." This sound gives them the reputation for having no bark.

Chihuahua is one of the smallest dog breeds. The breed's standard weight is 4–6 pounds. The Chihuahua's origin is linked to Mexico and may go as far back as 100 A.D. The breed name comes from a region in Mexico later named Chihuahua.

German Shepherds originated in Germany in the later 1800s. In rural Germany, they were first used for herding and protecting sheep. Modern-day German Shepherds have taken on different jobs such as acting, serving in the armed forces, and becoming service dogs.

Mixed breeds like Hoppy do not fit into any of the official dog breed categories and are usually not intentionally bred, although the world has hundreds of millions. Boomer, Peanut, and Doogie are examples of purebred dogs, which have been purposely bred by humans.

To find out more fun facts about dog breeds, go to the American Kennel Club website: www.akc.org.

Molly's British:

Blimey! Exclamation such as Oh, my goodness!

Clear off! Get lost!

Cheerio! Friendly goodbye

Musical Terms:

Pitches: Sounds that are the building blocks of melodies

Notes: Another term for pitch and used to refer to symbols on notated music

Rhythm: Movement and pulse of music through time

Melody: Pitches that form the main part of a song.

Accompaniment: An instrumental or vocal part that supports the principal voice or instrument

A Hard Nut to Crack

Boomer's Tales: Book 2

A Preview

I jumped up on my hind legs and yipped, "Throw it!"

"Fetch!" Chloe said. The fuzzy red ball whizzed over my head.

My tail wiggle-waggled; I ran to get my favorite toy.

"Drop it!" she said when I brought it back to her. I placed it at her feet.

"Sorry, boy! This has to be a short game." Chloe gave me a treat. "Mrs. Lee wanted me to stay after school to g-give me some music for the end-of-the-year convocation."

Nana Weathers looked out the door and called, "Hey, you two, come in now. Dinner's almost ready."

"Boomer, I'll race you to the door," Chloe said.

Okay, but we know who's going to win. Four paws are always better than two.

When we got inside, Chloe went to wash her hands. The doorbell rang. Excited, I yipped.

"It's okay, Boomer. I've got it," Nana Weathers said.

When she opened the door, Robbie, our friend, shouted, "Hoppy's gone! I've looked everywhere, but I can't find him. Mom went to the grocery store, and while she was gone, I let Hoppy out to potty in the backyard. I went back in the house for a few minutes to finish up some homework on the computer. When I came back outside and called him, he didn't come. The fence gate was open."

Chloe came out of the bathroom. "W-What's wrong?" she asked.

Robbie told her and added, "When Mom returned, she helped me look for Hoppy. We went through the neighborhood shouting his name and whistling. No luck. Now it's getting dark and I'm really worried." Robbie pulled out a red and yellow striped piece of paper from his pocket. "I found this candy wrapper on the ground outside the fence. I don't eat this kind of candy. Why would it be on the ground?"

He handed it to Nana Weathers. She said, "Boomer, come." She put the wrapper to my sniffer and let me sniff, sniff. I smelled Chloe's favorite. She loved anything with chocolate like chocolate cake, chocolate brownies, and chocolate sprinkles on top of ice cream. I also smelled Robbie, grass, and a human smell I didn't know. Nana Weathers showed the wrapper to Chloe and asked, "Do *you* eat this kind of candy?"

"No, Nana."

"Well, Boomer's gotten a good sniff, which may prove useful. I'm going to put this away in a safe place for now." I padded after Nana Weathers into the kitchen. She reached into the drawer where she kept sandwich baggies and put the wrapper into one.

"Boomer, I'm going to put this wrapper on the top shelf of this cabinet so it doesn't accidentally get thrown away. Let's go see if we can give Robbie some reassurance about Hoppy. He's so upset."

When we walked back into the hallway, I heard Chloe say, "I'm sorry about Hoppy. I want to h-help you find him."

Leaping up on my hind legs, I yipped, "Me too!"

Nana Weathers said, "Robbie, we all want to help you find Hoppy. I know how upsetting it is when a pet is missing. When I was a girl, my yellow-striped tabby cat, Pinky, disappeared for two weeks. I looked and looked for him. One day I was out riding my bicycle around the high school with my best friend when I heard a loud meow. Pinky came up to me like I'd been the one who was lost and was now found."

Chloe laughed. Then she said to Robbie, "I've got an idea. Since tomorrow is S-Saturday, talk to your parents about all of you c-coming over to our house for a b-breakfast meeting. We can make a plan for finding Hoppy if he isn't home by morning."

"Yes, we'll form an official Hoppy search party," Nana Weathers said.

Robbie smiled. "Thanks. I knew you'd help. That's why I came over. Although Hoppy is frisky, I don't think he'd run away, even if the fence gate was open."

About the Author

Christine Isley-Farmer's first book in her series, "Boomer's Tales," features a Cavalier King Charles Spaniel as the story's narrator. Christine loves this dog breed and has owned three Cavaliers. She encountered her first Cavalier, Fleur, while performing with the Harrisburg Opera. She was captivated by the big brown eyes and gentle, lively nature of the breed. Her present Cavalier, Dylan, likes to walk with her, chew on his favorite treat-stuffed Kong toy, and snuggle next to her in a recliner. Christine, a classically trained singer who has sung professionally in the United States and Europe, has also been a voice teacher. The stories in opera and song have fascinated and inspired her. The power of stories and music's healing qualities have woven their way through her life and have found voice in *Finding My Yip*.